Ronald M. Schernikau
translated from the German by Lucy Jones
with an afterword by Ben Miller

SMALLTOWNNOVELLA

UGLY DUCKLING PRESSE | LOST LIT #36

SMALLTOWNNOVELLA
by Ronald M. Schernikau

First Edition, Second Printing

ISBN: 978-1-946604-41-5
Library of Congress Control Number: 2025940355

Lost Literature #36

Ugly Duckling Presse
The Old American Can Factory
232 3rd St #E-303
Brooklyn, NY 11215
uglyducklingpresse.org

SMALLTOWNNOVELLA

Love song from a bad time

We were not on friendly terms
But we made love all the same.
As we lay together and kissed
You were further than the moon.

And if we met at the market today
We might fight over a pair of fish:
We were not on friendly terms
As we lay together and kissed.

—bertolt brecht

i am afraid. am female, am male, double. feel my body moving away from my body, see my white hands, my eyes in the mirror, i don't want to be double, who am i? want to be myself: male, female, i only see white. i face myself, want to reach out to myself, stretch my arms towards myself, where am i? i see, kiss, and wrap my arms around myself and become one. lea appears once, then again, and finally he is conscious and notices. b feels: he's lying in bed, it's morning, his room is a blur, he tries to take it in, feels his head moving, doesn't try to steer it. has no hope that today will be a good day, fuckinggettingup, fuckingschool, fuckinglife. his mother usually gets on his nerves, trying to wake him with the same words and phrases she has used for years, in that same tone of voice. there's no escaping her love, which makes her wake him so tenderly that it drags on unbearably. his coming round, collecting himself, and crabbiness are just reactions to her attempt to delay reality. if he tells her at lunch that he was late for school again, that lat teased him, that lenkel let him flirt with her instead of apologizing, or lehm gave him another lecture on his constant sloppiness, she says: perhaps we should get up earlier, or she just accepts it. getting up earlier is impossible if only because mornings would then be dull, and a dull start colors the whole day. even throwing back the covers is an effort, and so he doesn't, certain she will give him another warning. the patient stage of her waking-up routine is already past; now she is ratty, and soon she will seem adamant. when she gives up, he'll get up. after he forces himself to open his eyes, his mind clears. glancing at his schedule pinned to the wall, he runs through his school day. he can't read what it says but he has colored each subject and almost knows the sequence of classes by heart. still, to be sure, he has to outwit his short sight. b loves his glasses: they're his constant companion and have been through all he's been through for the past two years. he is proud of them when he comes in from the rain and has to clean them, or when they fog up in the shift from cold to warm and he goes blind. now he kisses them, murmurs, sings, does an operetta: i am a slave to you my whole life long. b sits up, swings out of his bed, the mattress has shifted. he stands up, turns around, sees black spots before his eyes for a moment: low blood pressure. he hears his spine crack as he bends backward. he staggers into the hallway after pulling on his jeans, goes to the closet, and stands there uncertainly: shirt time is decision time. eventually he grabs any old thing, throws it on and goes to the table where she's been calling for a while: i'm sitting down already! two eggs await him, one in the schnapps glass with the gold rim, the other lying next to it, and his cup of coffee, into which he tips milk and three heaped teaspoons of sugar. he hears himself say: double latin first thing. the coffee is a testimony to her maternal care: a lot of love, a little cocoa. lea has influenced his taste from a young age, and these days he can't eat anything that isn't sweet; if that's not an option, then he'd rather eat something bitter or sour. as he stirs his coffee, he thinks back to his dream, finding it hard to remember. this, as always, makes him try even more, which in turn makes it even harder. his dreams don't usually come back to him, only sometimes at school, perhaps during break, but often in some class, which he then hates even more. his thoughts make him hot; he wants to run off, get away, completely immerse himself in last night's dream, just to be alone, just to process it in peace. but he's either sitting across from his mother whom he calls by her first name, or with a bunch of bored teenagers who are probably thinking about their dreams, their girlfriends, their last jerk-offs or good grades, unless they happen to be doing homework for their next class. if b stormed out, down the steps, and across the yard to the toilets, his dream would vanish and he would curse, wait a while, then go back upstairs. he knows what's in store once he's drained his cup of coffee: orders, warnings, instructions, all sickeningly trivial and familiar, packing his school bag, doing his daily bathroom routine to constant shouts from outside the door, forgetting everything from brushing his teeth to remembering his glasses, money, books, keys, and notes. b slowly savors his second egg, and his mother worries that he'll never be able to leave home, which makes it necessary for precisely this reason, strengthening b's longing to do so: when he no longer needs to delay anything, he'll change. b stands up, dithers about for four seconds, then goes into the bathroom. he hates his morning ejaculations, his well-practiced, beautiful body, his hair in the mirror, his nose that, once you know, you can see was broken, jumping on the trampoline at school, his eyebrows that join, his mouth with its full lips, the two incisors that flash when he smiles, and the hair on his chin, so meager that he's ashamed of it. what he loves are his upper lip, the pubescent fuzz on it that's having some success, and the large, pale-red tip of his cock in his right hand. he overlooks his big, sky-blue eyes, only aware that they are much more expressive with make-up, and that his long eyelashes only do the trick when he bats them slowly, which can come across as trampy, or vampy, or campy, or dumb. when he comes out of the bathroom, lea is standing there in her coat though she knows perfectly well he needs another ten minutes. he snaps this at her, has of course no idea where his latin book is, reads the headlines of yesterday's paper in passing, in order to confirm once again that he's not alone in the world, however with lea, who follows him everywhere. he picks up his german textbook from the floor but the notes and booklet fall out, causing a further delay of about fourteen seconds that makes them both even more impatient. digging around among the coats: it's too cold for the black jacket either with the palestinian scarf or grey silk kerchief and his coat is too well-cut to be accepted by the slackers whose dress code is no guarantee: cdu-party key rings can hang on low-slung jeans too. he takes his cardigan that won't keep him warm either but which he likes because his protest pins fit between two rows of stitching: and armed with these pins, he is strong. b pulls on a thick sweater to wear underneath, loops a belt around his waist, looking like a girl from the back, reaches into the key box as he goes past and walks on ahead. long, dark entrance hall, doors on either side, lift, glass door, seventy letter boxes, seventy doorbells. it's a fine, clear winter's day and from afar the bells are ringing. they cross a field and his mother enters the six-story building in front of them, the hospital, which is the workplace of all the tenants behind them. b's mother is a nurse, they live in the apartment block for healthcare staff, and just now b is reaching the intensive care unit that's used as housing because of bad planning, and where his classmate lives, whose mother is a doctor. b taps his fingers on the window pane where, on the other side, leyla is just putting on a blouse and looking in the mirror. she turns round, sees him, laughs, makes a sign he doesn't understand and leaves her room. b hears tchaikovsky's first piano concerto coming from somewhere. leyla comes out with lutfiye, kisses him on the cheek, asks: hey, how are you? and takes his hand. you're wearing my shirt today, says b and gets a smiling yes as a thank you for noticing. the two sisters are a head shorter than him; the three of them look funny in the big wardrobe mirror when they visit. have you practiced for the vocabulary test? lutfiye asks, concerned. she's cramming for her final exams, and sometimes quizzes him on the stuff they have to learn. b laughs, asks: what for? he takes solidarity for granted yet expects disapproval of his displays of anarchy. leyla talks to lutfiye in their native tongue—turkish—and b walks along next to them, not the center of attention, annoyed, then reminds himself it's just a habit or silliness. they go past the high-rise hospital building where a woman jumped from the top floor not long ago. they stay clear of the faint bloodstains on the grass, and have to climb over a chain as there's no official path here. after b has climbed over it, leyla holds it up and limbos under it, while lutfiye goes round. like every morning, b feels the advantage of his one meter ninety stature. but i don't look brawny, he thinks, just gawky. they cross the main road, turn into the small street, thereby walking around the schoolyard that is bordered on both sides by the sidewalk, and enter the building, a school route of five minutes. people stand outside the entrances, waiting for the bell, smoking their first cigarettes, and having their first moan. b says hello!, loses the two girls to some group or other, goes over to renate to whom he owes a mark from yesterday, gives it to her, chats. what've you got now? renate asks. latin, b answers, because since they started choosing their own subjects, each of them has a different schedule. b pulls out his latin book and looks at the vocabulary for the first time. the meanings are precise. there is only one word—*bonus*—that covers the meanings of good, decent, affluent, and conservative. and *liberalis* means both outspoken and generous. when the bell rings, they linger a while, then go into the classrooms. b walks up a few stairs to room twenty-two in the old building, says a few hellos!, throws a few silent looks, arrives, goes in, and sits down next to laura. hey stupid, how ya doing? she greets him, like every morning. ach, same as ever. she gives him an invitation to her youth mass in the village church on saturday, which they have spent ages preparing. she knows he'll come, doesn't try to persuade him, just presses the dog-eared invitation retouched with felt tip pen into his hand and says: you coming? b says: sure, and smiles. she tells him about her work; he shares her enthusiasm for courses and successes, and the youth work done by the local small-town pastor, which means a great deal in a society that encourages everything, just not social behavior. b goes up to the blackboard, takes the chalk, and writes in childish scrawl: those who don't risk danger, are killed by it. someone calls out from the crowd: so, you wanna be a philosopher someday, or what? and the ones who have read it laugh, and b joins in. they're sitting on the tables, and when the latin teacher walks in, they sink into the chairs that their feet are still on, no longer noticing the regular outrage of the man up front. lat pretends to be hip, but they all know that this newfangled behavior puts him on edge. lat is mr banks, who has a governess called mary poppins, and who announces, singing: "tradition, discipline, and rules must be the tools! without them: disorder, catastrophe! anarchy!" someone who has spent his whole career translating biased reports on infantry, encampments, and attacks, has a worldview infused with true values: there are the diligent and the lazy, cowards and statesmen, orators and masses. only in these guises is a man reactionary and progressive. the world of latin texts is ruled by the hardworking and the strong, who let youths vie for their favor, a circumstance that, as lat indignantly comments, was simply due to the prevailing notions of morality at that time: a rare caveat. if people never learn about contexts, how can they assume there were any? nobody around b seems to notice the cruelty of lat's example sentences to illustrate various grammatical rules. but it's important whether he killed his mother beforehand or was right in the middle of it! the leader saw that the soldiers loved him! he considered him a friend! and on cicero: the text is written for intelligent romans, not fishmongers! the worst part is the phrase: with dead certainty! repeated three or four times a class. next to him, peter is trying to set fire to his textbook under the desk, perhaps testing the school curriculum's resilience. b escapes by swapping notes with laura. now and again, he's picked to recite rows of pronouns and gets it wrong, of course. lat thunders: learn, you atreuses! and nobody dares ask what it means. b is done with lat who regularly goes over time and doesn't give them a break during the double class.

when they're outside, the conversations start: see that film on tv last night? crazy! the way he kept whacking him in the guts and shouting: kindergarten! and everyone dead at the end. was a bit cheesy to start with but otherwise: hellyeah! it's the second re-run and they're still none the wiser, b thinks melodramatically. some go to the kiosk, which only survives thanks to them: here they chat, drink coke, eat chips, rum balls, or trail mix, and buy or bum ciggies, and it's a trading post for scroungers and their hash. the following incidents threaten to escalate into utter chaos, writes the principal in a handout that is passed around: every break time, the school is turned into a traveling circus. doors, tables, and chairs are demolished, and nobody takes the slightest responsibility. we would be justified in locking the toilets for reasons of hygiene: cisterns are blocked, rolls of toilet paper are shoved down drainpipes, toilet seats are dirtied in the most revolting manner, paper towels are set alight, etc. the windows have been equipped with special security braces. in many cases, these braces have been removed in order to open the window fully. the conduct of students and motorists in front of the building is a cause for concern. it is merely a matter of time before the first accident forces us into the harsh reality of an administrative investigation. please therefore advise your classes once again that all students below the tenth grade are forbidden to leave the schoolyard at break times. i propose to the school committee that infringements should be penalized with up to three days' suspension as i cannot otherwise bear responsibility for student safety. to underscore the seriousness of the situation, i am notifying the municipal administration and parents about this letter. i also request that all homeroom teachers read out my directives in class!

despite the mostly amused reaction to the handout, profits fall. the only people who still hang out on the schoolyard during breaks are those who have to chug a beer at half past nine in the morning to get through the day. that's what school teaches you: if everything's shit in the first place, then just run away from it all, but don't conform, no matter what! resistance is bullshit, doomed to failure from the start, so not worth the bother. you're better off with a beer or a joint. and someone who's just toking on one and whose laughing "nuclear power? no thanks!" pin twinkles on his jacket, smiles at b, who says: if we just smoke enough, they'll soon stop with their nukes. the guy laughs back. b goes into the new building, advanced german with lenkel, counts toward final grades. at the beginning, he told the others she made him want to take her hand, breathe a kiss onto it, and with barely mustered self control, stammer the words: "dear lady, i honor thee." lenkel just brings it out in him. she's fashionable, small, and overweight. in any case, nothing helps her much, not the discreet lavender nail polish nor the handbag, watch, and ear clips to go with every outfit: the trouble the woman goes to is just staggering. b once watches her reading *petra* women's magazine during a class test and can hardly finish writing his paper because he's laughing so much in sympathy for this woman whose face reveals everything: her frustration, the odds stacked against her.

renate is giving a presentation. b asks if there's a handout: will you be putting out copies? laura prods him: more like putting on a show. the source of renate's reading is *directions in german literature*, published by ullstein, quote: raabe's historical awareness leads to moral and political awareness since, for him, history never merely represents *heimat*, a haven to which one can retreat from oppressive events in the present, but also imprisonment in the temporal, to which one is forever bound in hope, fear, and blessing. this is the source of his life-affirming worldview, which, while not radiantly devout, is defiantly brave! cabaret's so simple: all you have to do is quote. what directions has the history of literature taken? after the epoch of sentiment comes the epoch of rationality, then sentiment again, and so on. very good. it's unclear which one we are currently in. the nature of our society and literature are also unclear; everything, in fact, is unclear. we can only search for answers. class papers have to be searching too, otherwise they're ideology and therefore bad. a finished interpretation is not allowed, evaluations are not part of the assignment, but feelings while reading and essays are. literature has little to do with politics; the political writers were all terrible without exception. renate, please carry on! docked yourself a point there, sweetie, bad luck! b says to himself scornfully: walked straight into that one! you're done for! and murmurs: some people hex warts; we're hexing this poem. you're very coquettish, do you know that? lenkel says, as they go through his last german essay. after her careful and clever editing of his first paper, she reached the end of her tether when she read b's second wildly disjointed, ranting thought-frenzy. below it she writes an angry, rude comment, and grades his paper with one point for his political commentary, not his literary exposition. this is certainly new. so far none of the german teachers whose job it is to police him have let their apolitical standards slip. each one freaked out when he applied literary truth to the system as a whole. abstraction is not only *not* part of the assignment, it is also graded harshly as garbage, ideology, radicalism, deplorable. what lenkel calls coquettish is precisely this subversiveness because she's not used to it. what does strauss have to do with jean-paul? and franknorbert warns him, that's dangerous! when he flirts with lenkel, or draws attention to her slipping hemline, or, when b shouts loudly, ah, the worldview of german teacher lenkel! because she says böll doesn't deserve the nobel prize, or when he complains that she should remain objective when declaring that the novel is dead. she'll take offense!, whispers franknorbert. is he right, the first of them to ride a motorbike? how much tolerance and self-criticism can this smiling woman take, who may not agree with the anti-radical decree, and who likes it when he tells her things she doesn't know, and swaps books with him. his previous german teacher was not afraid to say to his face: keep your mouth shut until you've passed your final exams, then you can do what you like, don't throw it all away. and at college, someone will come along and say: get your phd first, pass your exams first, fit in, grow up, become like us. b is grudgingly given good grades. the teachers write below his texts: your essay displays your usual brilliant grasp of the subject that strives to get to the heart of the issue, but it appears to be beneath you to do the proper work. once again, this essay suffers from stylistic mannerisms at the expense of objectivity. the objectivity of the topic requires a dry tone to match, no emphatic wording please. the aphorisms in your essay have cost you many points, because they impede an understanding of what i believe are your very profound views. the presentation of your arguments is detailed and interesting, but occasionally, as you even admit at one point, a little biased. occasionally? always! you bet! he screams at everyone who teaches him. and cries when the geography teacher stands in front of the students and yells: socialism is the biggest scam of humankind! he cries at home so that nobody sees, and never wants to go back. if he criticizes a poem, there's mockery from the teacher at the front of the class: too western and decadent for you, hmm? stupidity can be disproved and perhaps simply ignored, but when you're a school student and subject to it? laura slides a note over to him: how you doing? all right i hope coz i'm not, like whenever renate's giving a presentation. the bell goes, lenkel leaves, b calls after her, today your lavender day? and she smiles. b holds up laura's letter, calls out to renate: look, laura wrote me a letter, i'll read it out. laura tries to grab the note but b reads out loud: how you doing? all right i hope. laura laughs, lowers her head, says: oh no. coz i'm not, b finishes and gives laura her note back. renate has no idea what's going on and laughs. laura whispers, you idiot. they get up, b pulls on his jacket, fetches his sandwiches and pack of juice, and goes downstairs with martina. she says, jeez, that was boring as ever. and kinda wishy-washy, b replies. he prefers agitprop, word of mouth propaganda. knit it yourself? b asks liane about her new pullover and she says, my mum made it, d'you want the pattern? and b does. she asks, what wool would you use? pink and very fine, then i can hang a locket in the cleavage! and liane groans loudly: oh boy, not even girls wear those. i'm emancipated, b lies once to this happy group, and someone says: you can be proud of that. yeahyeah.

is it obvious when b's gaze follows people around the school yard? there goes leif, under his gaze. how does it seem to someone who's watching? pathetic? cheesy? b has only known leif a year, since they were sent to this school with another hundred and twenty students. here it's up to fate whether old friendships fizzle out, firm up, or fall apart. isn't it a high price to pay in exchange for a couple of—quote unquote—free subject choices, limited anyway by a shortage of staff and rooms, pay rates for higher-level teachers, and elbows used at faculty meetings to fight for the best courses? what does it come down to? says b, making himself unpopular at german faculty meetings: image, age, or beauty? what are the criteria for assigning courses to teachers? what happens to free subject choices for students when the worst teacher offers the most courses, and there's no option but to fill them? leif sits in one of these futile courses, and b watches him, tries to get close during break by making jokes and eventually sits next to him in the semicircle during the double art class twice a week. b spends his time at school assessing people, obsessing over leif, accompanying him to the kiosk, watching as he takes the coke b has bought and puts it to his lips, then passes it on to his girlfriend. b keeps to himself, patiently listening to boring speeches about chemistry or wines or—the ultimate!—motorcycles. when b's class is canceled unexpectedly, he sees leif standing with some others at the kiosk and they have their first conversation, though b suddenly feels watched and insecure, like the others when they're around girls. he hangs around and joins in the conversation about the twelfth graders' trip among other things—either to berlin or a skiing hut or the french border. all one hundred and twenty students in the senior grades can choose where they go, and when b finds out that he's going to berlin, like leif, he says: fuckyeah. b will tell leif about his dread of cliques: of yours, he'll say, who will stick together on the trip and jerk me around; i'll run to the girls for cover. and he won't follow the advice leif gives him when they're alone: hit back when they don't expect it! b doesn't want to. are you too weak, asks leif, or what? maybe, says b, but more to the point, i don't want to be strong, or athletic, i don't feel like hitting anyone. b has often been beaten up and the only self-defense he's ever dished out was a slap across the face. b had seen it in a film and was proud of it, but the guy on the receiving end said: just like a girl. don't take it to heart, leif consoles him, all manly, perhaps even with a trace of understanding and tenderness in his voice. or so it seems to b, who says: i can run away when it happens in the school yard, but in berlin, with all of us stuck in a group? leif even has to justify to his clique why he says hello to b; his mates don't pick up on much but they do have eyes. i say hello to other guys even if i don't hang out with them, he says. liane plays go-between between b and the gang, telling him the latest news, and their latest remarks. of course they seem rough compared to the sheltered life he lives at home, and that's why it is impossible for b to infiltrate the group, or first just fit in, which he'd have to do to convert them, to overcome their prejudices against long coats, for a start, coats that don't look like parkas or wax jackets. liane takes care of all this for him and her reports keep him upbeat. she delivers notes pushed across tables or reports brief remarks made in the schoolyard which have lasting effects. and b laughs brazenly, unexpectedly, at things they take for granted, like: you looking for a punch in the face? he wants to get beneath leif's macho posing, thinks that by ribbing him a few times, the jockish veneer will crack. what makes b follow leif around? the challenge? a secret desire to be like him? or like the other machos? and what about the other way round? leif wants to study something that pays well: a dumb job is automatically fun if the cash is right! and this is the kind of guy b shares a passenger car with on the class trip, putting up with the normality he's always fled from. in sport, for example, he uses ploys and favors, like notes from doctors he knows, because he can't bear watching how sweaty boys act together: the way they jostle each other during team games and always pick on the smallest guy, which is the ultimate in attention. and group showering becomes an ordeal, because towels draped around youthful loins are just curtains for the play: whose is the biggest, and who hides his pride the most brutally? the one who's always shooting off his mouth can sometimes afford to grab another between the legs: painful but just kidding! of course, and so fucking manly. this must be how imperial armies and torturers got it on: together yet apart, touching allowed only after pointing out the lack of women. i would puke if they picked on me. in the locker rooms, major combat rages more openly than elsewhere. this is where men are trained to beat up faggots and rape women. this is where the systematic destruction of happiness takes place. these guys take on a double portion of unhappiness from their fathers: they have to be manly so that nothing changes and at the same time, they must pretend to be happy, fixated on the next fuck or jerk-off, with no possibility of escape. when b backs off, they're pissed, they don't understand, they say: he's the other way. b knits in the passenger car of the train, natters to leyla and the others about knitting patterns, v-necks, and color combinations, says no to leif's beer, doesn't want to be drunk on the first day in the big city. needs it, but not with these people, thank you very much! cognac in his coffee gives him a rush, helps him say to the world: fuck your problems! or: venceremos! b stares out of the train window, takes measure of this fleeting happiness, then someone makes him jump by handing him a *brigitte* magazine into which he escapes. but then this form of escape feels even less perfect, and so he withdraws by joining in, getting drunk after all, stuck in this absurdly funny city with a group of twelfth graders whose only cultural skill is to take the piss out of each other, and to go on one long drinking binge. but after the group blackout every night, the following scene takes place: leif remembers, catches up with b after breakfast, takes him up to his room, says: you were drunk yesterday. b guesses what's coming and says: weren't you? is excited, hears: yeah, you said something about being in love. ah, b laughs, lovely topic, don't you think? with me. excuse me? with me. you said i was wonderful and beautiful and you were, with me. and b: i was drunk, i'd been reading all day, having thoughts, my feelings were all mixed up. are you gay? yes.

because of course b is gay. he hangs out in the schoolyard with the girls, looks around, says hello, stands still, and is gay. ladies and gentlemen, you are now listening to the program, "a homosexual is always suspect." johanna müller reports on prejudices against a minority. we will discuss which prejudices we hold against homosexuals and how they deal with them. we have recorded the live reactions of five homosexual men to comments made by two heterosexual men. b has a large circle of friends and through a gay men's support group, he's asked to take part in a talk at a local radio station with an impressive restroom, big enough to dance in. let's see if i use the ladies' or the men's room!, he announces, and his joke lands. he flirts with the program director who writes a literary column for the *stern* journal and who "listened with warmhearted sympathy" as he reassures them after the recording. they are sitting in the radio station canteen and b is bored by the others' whispers—did you see? look at him! isn't that?—because he doesn't know any of them. on the way here, he met martina and, in a bold mood, told her: hey, we're doing a show, five gays in a studio. why you? well, because. oh, right. and she'll sit by the radio like everyone else from school and afterwards everyone will know. and if someone says, i don't advertise that i'm gay, but i don't hide it either, that's too easy. perhaps purposely wearing the pink triangle, the symbol for gays in concentration camps, is just an odd overstatement of our own isolation, but defamation comes in all kinds of forms—helplessness, embarrassment, laughter, or therapy. how normal is b? he's encouraged to wear makeup: is that the new red champagne color that's in fashion? he asks lenkel during a test, pointing to her fingernails. no, she laughs, says: if you like it, why don't you wear it? it would definitely suit you! b is stunned, and laughs back, saying, nah, come on! lenkel replies, why not? doesn't bother me, anything goes these days! b says, if only, and carries on writing. buy it, suits you, says laura, when they're shopping downtown. this? it's for girls. that's silly, says laura, like who cares. and b gets bolder, pins rhinestone brooches on his jacket, puts his hair back with leyla's black plastic hairband that goes with his ladies' watch. ha ha! look, a boy with a ring! yells b's cousin who's sitting on his lap in the streetcar. so what? says b sullenly. do you want one too? and the little girl jumps down, crowing as she runs to her mother: mommy, mommy, he's wearing a ring! yeah? her mother laughs awkwardly, apologetically, looks at him and quickly away again. mothers, do the following test if you want to know whether a gay man has just walked past: does your victim sway his hips when he walks? is he dressed in the latest fashions? does he have a frustrated look on his face? your average gay man looks like a jilted woman, having been kicked around since the hair on his legs started growing. not only the mass media make sure of this, but parents and psychiatrists do, too. when *stern* writes that not all homosexuals perform anal sex, the journal is trying to defend an honor that doesn't exist. the bourgeois defense of the honor of those who reject bourgeois morality can only be bourgeois—absurd, in other words. a gay man's honor is like that of the middle-class man: he smiles no matter what and gets upset when his little cap slips: is that honor? b is still thinking about this when a guy walks past. if b grabbed his arm and said, come on, i'm up for it!, he might get a punch in the mouth. the element of surprise can't overcome upbringing. b thinks about this much too often and probably misses out. when b sees the guy stop in front of a store window, he goes to stand next to him, and watches him in the windowpane. the guy notices, but a smile doesn't work: they part. sometimes b practices smiling in the mirror because it so often doesn't work. now, if *he* isn't gay then i don't know who is! thinks b, when he spots a boy sitting across from him on the train. blond, fashionable—the frames of his glasses! slim hands that are browsing through his wallet, sorting through photos, looking at his own driver's license picture; then he pulls out a flowered notepad, arranges himself in the corner, the back of his hand on his cheek. something flashes on his left ring finger! well, that's for sure, he definitely is! no makeup, true, and no earring, which b sometimes longs for, but that little neck chain! his crossed legs! the way b does too, because he is, too. after ages, the guy notices b staring. now he's staring back: he's older than b first thought, and cuter. soon their relationship will be over. b arrives at his stop, will the guy get out too? b stands up, throws on his things, always keeping his eyes on him, but the other guy makes no sign of getting up. by the time b reaches the exit, he's given up hope. of what anyway? then the guy comes after all and walks the same way as b until his girlfriend meets him, and he gives her a peck on the cheek. and as they walk away, b notes: the straights are getting more effeminate these days, too.

as the vagaries of desire will have it, b has fallen for someone in the schoolyard again, without making it obvious, of course. b stands with some group, and sees leif. b sticks his straw into his triangular carton and sucks on it. the young socialist from tenth grade appears out of nowhere: gimme a sip? if you gimme a kiss! says b. the young socialist gives him one and helps himself. the bystanders laugh, and b doesn't know what else to do except feign ecstasy, caricaturing himself, as if bowled over. those standing around give him a bite of their sandwiches because he's always hungry. they drink from his can of coke which is twice as expensive at the kiosk as in the supermarket, and admire all his new pins. stop the neutron bomb! lennart reads, pats him on the shoulder, says, sensible attitude. get that off, says laura to a boy and leyla says, i have scissors, and together they detach the west german flag from his parka. bell's gonna go, says b and the bell goes. on the way up, b ribs a young kid, tugging on his t-shirt and saying to liane: how about we roast him? the kid turns round on the stairs, stares back, startled, he's two years younger than b and cute, says: there's not much meat on me. huh, thinks b, he even reacts, laughs, goes past him. good morning, jokes lennart behind him, my name is orgy and i always come when i'm least expected. b arrives on the top floor, now he has ethics, the substitute class for religious studies. he's never had religion, so is free compared to the others. instead, he's read sex ed books from a young age, the ones always meant for kids a grade higher than him. no hair or bodily fluids have taken him by surprise, rather, he's been amazed by his mother's innocence who doesn't seem to know what he uses his towels for. in the essay he's just received back which they're now going to discuss, b claims: knowledge is liberating and the cornerstone for an uninhibited attitude towards sexuality. lirus is reading verena stefan's book *shedding* with them, at the suggestion of a progressive student who belongs to an equally progressive clique. the guy smokes dope, dyes his hair, has nothing against his neighbor's homosexuality, nothing against leftists, and nothing against sensitivity or feminism. he's someone who takes an interest, someone b can talk to, who can discuss, and perhaps even listen. at some point, he'll have his hair cut short again like all the others, change his glasses and watch with every fashion, and we'll sort out his political views in time, too: if you're not a communist by seventeen, you have no heart, but if you're still one when you're thirty, you have no brains. b finds wishy-washy progressiveness creepier than downright naivety, which he can object to in conversations and essays. ansgar once told him about going round to franknorbert's, who asked him as he went in whether he was a communist and whether he would smash up his place. oh, how b laughed: what a misconception, what an ignoramus. being able to laugh when there's nothing to laugh about liberates b, who plays the fool at school and whose interactions often end in jokes or provocations that don't ask for a response, but seem to provide one. b has just written a good paper which they are now discussing in class after lirus arrives late. read it aloud, says lirus, and b does: he has nothing to lose. what this feminist, verena stefan, has experienced is conformist sexuality, which for me was only ever a transitional stage to my identity. my needs are not, and never have been, the ones that society finds acceptable. that's why, while i have never undervalued the significance of sexuality, i've always viewed it as fluid, simply because i exist: the world belongs to the perverse. because my feelings were different, i never felt the need to forget or exclude sexuality; it has always been far too clearly enmeshed in my overall circumstances for that. in the text, an experience is presented that the homosexual has to learn early on: that being homosexual, or even bisexual, is a no-go!, at best curable. regaining her polymorphous sexual identity is not a liberation, but a step toward it. b says this aloud and only then realizes to whom: his teacher, who is watching him. dress rehearsal for later. only now does b start worrying about this afternoon where he will be the subject of a school committee meeting to talk about the incident, which is an invasion of privacy. it's a mystery to me how you're going to get through this, with two more years of school to go. how come? you look so fragile. the same old song. please don't push me into the role of poor, pathetic creature, okay? he begs, because he's affected by the others' moods and can do without melancholy right now, especially not from this older gay man from the men's support group sitting in front of him. b gets up, turns to someone else, stays there and doesn't listen. they are halfway through class now and he has barely followed the discussion, doodling arrows on the page of his open notepad in front of him, then joining them up with wavy lines that get closer and closer together until the pattern covers the edges and soon the entire page. now b starts to fill in the pattern so that no white touches a filled-in square. it's impossible but b tries with each new drawing. if b meets a new guy, his name appears in his notepad too, because b's in love and thinks about him all the time. flicking back a few pages, he's written: leif. b is feeling under pressure and when a nurse from the hospital boasts of her new hairdo: the competition never sleeps, b laughs, unnaturally loudly, realizing: that's me, forced to play along, i'll never get anything in life for free. in biology, because they don't have sex ed, b declares, gay men do the exact same thing as the ballet dancer on this stupid slide: they put on makeup, dress to attract attention, camp it up. and what's more, he adds, now very dramatically: we've all made them this way. boys traditionally expect to be catered to, so the girls put on the silliest get-up to stand out. and gay men do exactly the same, knowing for sure that it won't work. b sits down again and thinks: nothing is more self-destructive than the patriarchy ridiculing the conditions it has produced. one day, every six-year-old will laugh at this morality, and scientists will seriously doubt their ancestors' sanity: don't accuse gays of acting unreasonably in an unreasonable world! what's the difference between a thirty-six-year-old gay man and an eighteen-year-old girl? when it comes to innocence and its opposite? what b sees in the discos of both scenes is shockingly similar. there's someone dancing: short, teased, brown-gray sprayed hair, big clip-ons, plucked eyebrows, perhaps rouge. but: the eyes! eyeliner, eyeshadow, red mouth, contouring to accentuate the nose, a shirt subtly gathered at the waist in the latest style, fingernails to match; and on the left hand, a few obvious rings, on the wrist, a chain with heavy links, and tight jeans that accentuate the crotch, out of which peep black seamed pantyhose, slipped into high-heeled pumps. he's tuned into love's airwaves, people, from his head to his hollow back! have you ever noticed that women with overly-long, fake, polished nails can't make a fist? they're not meant to work, nor do anything creative, they're supposed to be useless things to look at and fuck, to make men feel validated and entitled, raised and dressed only to be lied to: you've got it easy! but: the bourgeoisie has ripped the sweet, sentimental veil off gender relations and has reduced them to monetary relations. man versus woman becomes everyone versus everyone else. the price of profit is the erasure of the dividing line between the sexes: blurring it doesn't work because the ink it was drawn in dried up long ago.

bourgeois avarice forces outlets to create expensive fashion for men too, drives holes into the earlobes of youths, drives women into the arms of hairdressers who cut their hair short, and huge bears into teeny shoes. david bowie is the desperate dernier cri of fashion moguls and the first proclamation of a new category of sex in which it won't matter that words are a fallacy: gender, why not bender? and marilyn monroe is just another woman in a series of drunk, overpowered blondes when arthur miller has her slurring at people in tight pants: "fags wear pants like that." because one fashion follows hot on the heels of another, and the in-crowd follows hot on the heels of the out-crowd, and that's why their new look follows hot on the heels of the old. the hotter half is gay and the remaining half tries ever more desperately to be as popular with the ladies as the first half is with each other. hello!, says b when he enters. i'd like a pair of jeans that fits well and is cheap too. the sales assistant says, don't we all. lovely, b says cheerfully. if the demand's that high, the supply must be phenomenal! the sales assistant gives him a pitying look. the only lasting side effect of this pure form of paying and being paid is that the choice of what to wear will broaden because fashion magazines won't manage to make new outfits for everyone twice a year. and the more unconditional demand becomes, the less demanding people will become: today, anything goes! indian attire, workclothes, and nightwear are all worn on the street and hollywood stars wear glittery outfits to orphanages—wow, aren't we charitable!—and jeans to galas. b wears a dinner jacket to school and the baggiest of his own handknitted jumpers to the theater. and when he sees pictures of women with upswept hairdos in moscow and men with shaven necks, b knows: it's all about dialectics. when will b start wearing tight pants? when will b's shoes clack with each step? when will he sway his hips as he walks? when will his face show hurt or be hurtful? when will b get used to seeing men smirk even in his gay support group, where he's coddled and mocked because here, too, it's all peer and group and pressure, and no insight, not even shame. when will he get used to not having a leaflet thrust into his hand at demos because nobody dares go near him? when will b become aggressive, when eccentric, like the old guy from the association of victims of the nazi regime, whom he met near the changing rooms of the swimming pool, timidly watching the boys, ready to beat a retreat, on the lookout for innocents and trick-turners, and afraid of them? our triangle was pink, and b feels sick when he's attracted to a guy in the schoolyard wearing an iron cross. b calls werner and asks him if he's going to the market square in the city where the association of victims of the nazi regime has called a protest against the resurgence of fascism. meeting time is saturday at ten, for that i'll cut math! are other gays going to be there too? werner asks.

i don't want to have to pretend, i'll only come as myself, otherwise i may as well not come at all. werner's emancipated, also in the gay men's group. b doesn't want to hear the jokes about the butch guys on the opposite side and hangs up.

another five classes over, another free period, free but subject to recall, so no choice. what's free about a freedom that's like the pulse of a nerve with no off switch? in which dreams become more vivid and urgent and therefore more unattainable? in which there is only side-by-side boredom, or silent protest between books, and most people have more vinyl than books? in which we escape to discos, into any kind of subculture for teens, punks, intellectuals, political nerds, gays? my free time would be the opposite of idleness, b knows. and like everyone else, whether he hangs che on the wall whose picture is sold on every street corner, or bruce lee, he also knows it's the most desperate kind of protest. they can organize gigs or think long hair is cool, but it's important that they teach you: there's no alternative to idleness. b goes home, first waiting for leyla, but then going on ahead because he sees her dawdling. he says a quick hi to ansgar who cycles past: au revoir monsieur l'ansgar! and gets a smile in return: au revoir. b goes over to the hospital canteen, meets a couple of cleaning women, whom he timidly greets, and a few say hello back. how absurd is the phrase: generational conflict? how natural is b's relationship to women, to his peers, and how natural can it be? laura wants to study theology but doesn't have the money and will probably become a librarian. michael left school after tenth grade and is going to become an electrician. b asks him if he's happy, any regrets? he doesn't know. franz smokes and cuts class and will be one of the first waste products of this school. i'll stay here, says leyla when he asks her what she wants to do later on. liane has been seeing her boyfriend for almost half a year now and doesn't know whether she should sleep with him. monsieur l'ansgar reads and draws and makes music, and although his father is an architect, he never has much money; lucas is gay and when asked about his love life, he thinks only of his girlfriend in the small town, never about the man waiting for him in the big city; hartwig is new to the school and anxious and waits on the other boys: he runs to them when they click their fingers, nods, smiles, and doesn't ask questions. lena is retaking the year to avoid having to work. they're all seventeen, have never been beaten, have no neuroses, and won't have serious problems later, as long as unemployment among academics and university regulations don't get any worse, but in the end, only a few of them—. b does a deep dive into the world of labor, wage labor, pushing his back against the glass door to open it. the doorman doesn't respond to his greeting, afternoon!, like every day. he sees a mother squat down to greet her son and when he dials six-three-three on the patient's phone, he turns around and sees that the mother has tears in her eyes. at that moment, his own mother picks up. he says, hello, she: i'm coming. he hangs up and goes past the reception desk. the chief surgeon sends people with bleeding head wounds back here if their forms are not filled in properly, and the woman behind the desk, who sees him but doesn't say hello, danced with him at a work outing when he was twelve, and already too tall for her. no entry! access to the wards prohibited for children under the age of fourteen! set bag down, blue sticker with the peace dove turned to the back, hang up cardigan, say another afternoon!, take a tray from the counter on the left, then napkin, and knife and fork and spoon, d'you want soup, it's broth? take a big spoon, say hello to nurse adelgard again. and while he's being served, he weighs up where to sit down. if he's feeling mean, he sits, someplace with no space for lea, but that's not often. today next to frank who's studying here and has just come back from his uncle in south africa and who tells him: the blacks' only drawback is that they can't vote, that's all, and the tv reporters talk nonsense. no doctor will sit at their table, that's for sure, doctors have their own table; for b to sit at the nursing students' table is a rebellion, and the same goes for the staff table. b is welcome at his mother's table, but the doctors' table is the doctors' table, and the only drawback of not being one is: they can't sit at the doctors' table, that's all. b's mother arrives: hello there, young man, hello there, nurse lea, and she fetches her meal and asks: how was school? did they say anything? b sees there's shish kebab on his plate, the soup didn't reach his tastebuds. he shoves the skewer into his mouth, carefully bites on a piece of liver complete with onion ring, pulls the skewer out and thinks about leif: in berlin, he'll shower with the others after all, just to see how leif reacts. in berlin, those will be the only times they'll see each other naked. leif is attractive because he's approachable, and everything goes quiet in b, as if the volume has been turned down to create an intimate mood. b sometimes fantasizes about picking a boy, going up to him, embracing him, kissing, smiling at him afterwards. so far he's never done it and yet has done it countless times. i exist, b thinks, when a passer-by's gaze lingers on him. of course b likes the open expressions of innocent, short-haired boys but that soon turns to relishing their helplessness and insecurity. b, the master of ceremonies from *cabaret*, is demonic in his superiority, destroying the assured step of men, dragging them into filthy jokes or making them lower their gaze: a small island of self-assurance. and the dumb boys in b's class, who have to stand in the loge at the berlin opera because there are too few seats, can't even drop their role-playing when it comes to b, despite their huge capacity for self-repression; they usher him to a seat with the girls in the group who have the privilege to sit. b curses his dependence on men, a dependence on being maliciously mimicked—on himself, in other words. the world's lack of regard for him has taught b to overestimate himself: i am the center of the universe, the typical state of mind for the upwardly aspiring gay man. what actually happened? b wonders and sticks his fork into the processed rice: did leif take me seriously? what stopped him from beating me up? when they're with the others, they don't pay any attention to each other, have nothing to say to each other either, and are as different as any other. b has even stopped sharing everything with liane because he hadn't thought it would work out, somehow, that leif would come, to him and in his arms. what happens in berlin and later in their small town is just the usual teen mutual masturbation, without consequence for feeling, thoughts, or actions afterward, and without outward effect, because silence is a requirement for the normality they desire. we've become so alienated from ourselves that touching another person with your mouth feels more intimate than touching them with your genitals. and so, he kissed leif, but only timidly, afraid that the boy lying next to him might pull away. for what he lets b do to him in bed he forbids himself from doing, although prohibition is no longer necessary, as revulsion is always present. when b has finished eating, he takes his tray without saying goodbye, and slides it into the trolley provided. he takes his cardigan from the coat rack, glances at himself in the mirror, gives himself an encouraging smile, heads down the corridor and out, the reversal of lea's route this morning, across the lawn to their apartment block. he pulls out his key, first opens the mailbox, takes out the newspaper, then rides up in the elevator. that leif doesn't pull away from him means nothing. lack of resistance is not love, and as the english aristocracy allegedly say: "sexual intercourse is no means of social introduction." in the schoolyard that afternoon, leif doesn't turn up to meet him because he feels guilty, and b laughs, sure that he's innocent. lack of remorse, mrs massari, is what makes your son's behavior particularly problematic, says the school principal. for b doesn't just want to cum but to love, looks the other boy in the eye and self-assuredly demands openness—from himself, from the others, and ultimately from their parents. this doesn't happen the first time, or the second, but in the weeks that follow, when they're often lying together on b's bed, he grows braver, starts caressing leif in ways he isn't ready for, says words that leif finds awkward, and looks at him in a way that makes leif afraid of love, or what he thinks it is, and afraid of himself. i'm not gay! he screams the last time they meet, jumping up naked after a silent orgasm, and angrily starts to get dressed. b, who has lost his cool and his senses, looks in the direction where leif's eyes must be, grabs the nearest book, takes a huge swing, and lobs it at leif's right cheek. and in this b-movie scene, all goes quiet for a moment, and then b, who's hunched on the bed, begins to cry, and tries to stop leif from leaving, from splitting up, from not lying together anymore, and then leif finally sees what kind of guy he's dealing with: a lousy little fag, who knew nothing about the girls in leif's head, and nothing of the jokes in leif's clique. leif never comes back and b lies on his bed and can't even cry anymore. that same day, leif goes back to his unbroken home and tells his parents everything, and once their initial shock has passed, they immediately call b's mother, demand compensation and b's expulsion from school. lea's calm is unsettling enough as she listens to the irate account on the telephone, but even more, her question: why should my son be expelled? yours was just as involved? this is the ultimate denial of moral responsibility. but who seduced whom here? replies leif's gestator, a few decibels too loud, and hears: seduced? over many weeks? and these two attitudes are still driving the debate today: on the one hand, hysteria over the incident and the reaction towards it, and on the other, naïve astonishment at absurd moral norms. and the more public it becomes, the more desperate the hysteria grows. for b does everything to avoid an elegant solution, namely to pay damages—what a farce!—and to change schools. with his mother's solidarity and agreement, b mobilizes public opinion. he confronts the student committee, of which he is a member and who are uneasy about this; the parents' committee, who are appalled; and the gay men's group, who are delighted. and now b resolutely pursues what the father of his former lover wants to avoid at all costs—a public scandal! in doing so, he's risking a love he never had, but this becomes less and less important to him, the more he exposes how the small-town factions are all working against him. everyone seems to have been waiting for the opportunity to condemn him: the local newspaper, which scornfully abbreviates b's surname and sticks an exclamation point in parenthesis behind his position as student committee representative; lea's superiors, who advise her to publicly distance herself from the incident; and the school principal, who, in a conversation behind closed doors, advises b to change schools of his own free will, saying that his academic record certainly won't be improved by this incident. they all suddenly see themselves as guardians of an order in which sexuality does not exist: the magazines with lackluster photos and sex advice columns are only permitted because they make the progressive tampax and condom ads next to them more credible. but even these are nervously viewed by wide-eyed teachers, whose only comment on the depravity of their students is: but we didn't know that!, because otherwise they'd be forced not only to allude to sex but also comply with existing guidelines on sex ed. openness about sexuality is a random occurrence because of the ignorance of the school system, and where there is fear of discovering your own sexuality, soon sexuality itself is feared. how sad are the scenes with leif when he doesn't dare leave the house after they've been together, but doesn't want to stay with b either. and leif was able to denounce b because he only ever pleasures himself when they're together— "emptiness is me and you"—and so is less guilty than b who is in love or wants to be, tenderly and slow, at least that. and the teachers who speak to leif understand this too: just a pardonable slip-up, embarrassing, but seductions happen all the time. they even involve leif in deliberations about how b should be punished: do you think he'd do it again? or serially? do you think he's dangerous? how did he approach you? no woman is called in, not for either of them, and there's no fair treatment of the matter: we've got to deal with this very objectively! decide lirus, b's helpless tutor, who is responsible for him, and the principal; they want to solve the whole matter in private discussions. what kind of parents does he have? delving into b's permanent record, they discover: working mother, single—ah-hah!—and although talks with her are conducted in a suitably middle-class tone, there is visible revulsion at this family's sexual aberrance: she doesn't have a husband! to make matters worse, this woman does not see why homosexuality is any business of the school. she says: my private life is none of my employer's business either!, adding quietly: at least it shouldn't be. but what about our pedagogical mission, mrs massari! cries the principal, who normally talks quietly, as lea knows from his occasional appearances at parents' committee meetings, and who even pursues her at work, calling her to say: we have to intervene! of course, lea adds when sitting before him in his office, of course you would also intervene, if it were other feelings being expressed—ones that are not as easily suppressed, or that can't be suppressed at all. if your pedagogical mission is for real, you'll set up sentries in bedrooms, and not just at night of course. do you seriously think that your students learn better when they're unhappy? and that is b's mother's wrong move. at the next hastily called elections, she will be no longer be elected to the parents' committee. but until then, she makes full use of all the possibilities, asks teachers, students, and parents for legitimation, opinions, and solidarity, reads regulations and the students' newspaper, in which a gay joke suddenly appears. she does so much because a school committee meeting is scheduled to deal with the incident, a meeting that everyone wanted to avoid because it will only be embarrassing for them all. but b and also lea want it because it's the only way to put all doubt about morality and decent behavior aside. lea is a nurse, a single woman who has never understood why having a child means having to get married. she's middle-aged and self-confident, and thanks to her careful, serious activism, already a woman with a reputation. perhaps only now does she grasp what being gay means and how discrimination works. only now is she gradually realizing what has been the case for her son for a long time: that he wonders why there are no naked men on the covers of magazines, and why men reject him—when he is old enough to understand their rejection. why they push him off their laps onto the floor, grinning and saying: you're a boy, aren't you? he learns to grasp that what he used to do with girls write letters to them, go out with them, practice kissing—is no longer allowed with boys for some reason that he isn't aware of, and only later does he ask about sense and nonsense, about rationality and irrationality, in a world that can't even tolerate the most normal thing, but especially not the statistically abnormal; a world that thinks going for a shit between two courses of a meal is inconceivable and that tenderness is absurd. his careful attempts to express his feelings gave rise to liberal, uncomprehending looks from his mother, laughter at school and sudden, explicit dreams, which for years, or perhaps always, are about one thing: longing. as his awareness grows, b's gayness becomes an open secret with lea. they know about it without admitting it; ambiguity triumphs, at least that. and at the same time, his identification with the oppressor begins—to be a real man is a dream, only half-gay, only half, leave everything up in the air, provoke or be silent, then suddenly there is no in-between, therefore escape: to bury himself between the thighs of an american baseball player. and later, when in the most inconvenient moments, he's reminded of leif, he tosses and turns, groans, and curses everything he can think of right then. and it isn't love but a daydream that possesses him. for leif is the kind of guy who made b want to change schools years ago, the kind who found it tremendously funny to address b as fräulein, and at that age, it wasn't a quiet, ironic fräulein but one shrieked across the school yard, provoked by thirteen-year-old b's brightly colored scarves, provoking everyone, but especially those who took clique duties very seriously for fear of failing to fit in. b can understand this. it happened during a time when the high-school's token gay knew him and b rejected him with flirtatious horror: i'm not your little darling! while longing for him. he seriously thought about yelling i'm gay! in the face of an italian boy he met on vacation, although he only had a rough idea what that meant and wasn't sure it was true. now lea is baffled by his bravado and desire to enjoy life to the hilt. once, at the end of her tether during a quarrel, she says, i should have been stricter with you from the start. and then has to laugh. when they talk about fidelity, or when he sings *bye bye mein lieber herr* to her, she loves it and tells him so, smiling, amazed too, because she wonders whether everyone who is like him, is like him. when he learns about her question, she already has the answer, because she has met others like him and not like him, because she's danced in a gay disco and has watched movies in the cinema, profiting from the scant offerings of fassbinder, praunheim, and petersen. she lets him spur her on to rail against men, brutality, and egotism in general, and accepting things as they are in particular. she reads brecht: one often accuses homosexuals, when they talk to their friends, of camping it up and appearing ridiculous to those who consider themselves sober-minded. but do men behave any differently toward women? one should either be for campiness and displays of infatuation, or against them, regardless of where they occur. the tutors' meeting is short. after the briefest of testimonies from all the parties involved, everyone is told what they all already know, and the incident is deferred to the school committee without comment in the hope of deferring personal responsibility. b just manages to escape suspension. he'd have been granted it on request, but he goes to school, because he's the clear winner, even though his mood is more depressed each day, and while he manages to control himself one day, he explodes the next, while nothing else is normal: lenkel's smiles at his jokes are sad, hellos are superficial and forced, and the thirty or forty people in his circle are discreetly considerate, half-consciously convincing him that life is just jogging along as always. tomorrow, everything will fall apart once and for all, when the outcome of the school committee meeting is distributed by flyer, when teachers suddenly panic before taking senior grade classes, in which b is the subject of a discussion that would never have taken place, had spectacular events not occurred. when the next semester starts, leif will have left, discreetly, without a word and without any self-confidence either. so, b comes home, drained by this legal vampirism. school, the broken drug of school, b hears udo lindenberg singing, *madness and genius go hand in haa-and.* b drops his bag by the breakfast table, which is still cluttered with breakfast things, takes off his cardigan, and hangs it on the coat hook; it falls off, he picks it up and lays it over his chair, sits on it, takes off his white, hospital slip-ons, then, in a sudden fit of orderliness, takes them into the modern, windowless bathroom, throws them in the corner, lifts the toilet seat, finding the angle at which it stays up because the fluffy cover upsets the balance, and without it, looks sterile, resists a quick pleasuring, and glances in the mirror, for which he has to bend back because he's so tall and everything is hung so low. he smooths back his hair and unties his ponytail, smiles, lowers his head slightly, lifts his left eyebrow, special pose! b turns the light out when he leaves, when he's had enough of himself, goes into the living room, where he wants to see if there's anything on tv. leif: his looks. he tosses the newspaper aside when he realizes how little he can concentrate. masculinity, come-on, image: so, what he wanted. his appointments in the calendar: scm for school committee meeting. b laughs, b fights back, b takes up causes, b loves. who is leif? no homework today, insists b defiantly, to distract himself. leif is the only one considered violable, leif is human as opposed to masculine: vulnerable now, which inspires hope. b goes into his room. seeing in leif more than his own suppressed jockishness, more than his nice, short hair. who is leif? a member of the group, the joiner in persona, the longed-for happiness. open the window, lie down, glasses off. what was the beginning for b is the end for the other: when leif risked becoming like b, he gave up. i'm not gay! that's true. b has learned not to be able to fulfill expectations, and consciously, eventually, how to hurt on purpose. b has learned to hear footsteps. they echo back at him and become stares, they come towards him, and go past him. b has learned to hear that brief hesitation, that little inflection of making sure. the more obvious b is, the more obvious the others are. b stares back to unsettle them, fixes his gaze on them, turning the look in their eyes from stupor to derision, perhaps understanding to zero. so, walk blindly through the city, multiply their stares with imagined ones, disguise your certainty as uncertainty, your discouragement as courage. somewhere in leif's mind, this experience exists too, he knows it from his own reactions, from school, from his parents, drill is everything, everything is drill, it goes right through me. i'm seventeen and a man, and there's no need to crack the whip to teach me that the illusion of togetherness only exists as: having children, family trips, a car, vacation photos. a man exists as a small power plant that is decontaminated at home; he exists as his children's submissiveness, as success at work, as a tie, as a cock. if you can't come up with misogynistic stories during monday morning's banter, you're not a man. if you're not disgusted with yourself, you're a pig. b lies in his chaos. his room is his history. what leif can expect from life is blissful normality, achieved by doing absolutely nothing, no matter what. eyes shut. leif has moved, leif has broken out—only a little but already enough to fail. love, whatever that is: leif has tried it, and gave in when b touched him. the room in berlin after breakfast was filled with the two of them when they embraced. they didn't know what was happening, were both speechless and lost and very close. they went downstairs to the others in silence, separated from them by an experience which they tried to repeat for weeks: the experience of another. what eyelashes can be, a look and eyes closing, chapped lips on my skin. then, calm below, the feeling of being known. the desire to say: my love! darling. the hollow of the pillow, a pretty picture. who is leif? too bad, came too late, too early. a few chance moments have made leif realize how little divides him from another world. when the mask crumbles, the world crumbles; it moves, it changes. how close is leif to me? who had to decide, like me. who at least fought. who'll perhaps find it harder than b because his fight is over. can leif be happy? couldn't i live like that after all? einstein on the wall pokes out his tongue. b makes a face back. the end between me and leif is missing. what's left are a few moments, a slap in the face. no chance to talk it out and so on, no chance of mutual support, hoping, tenderness, fighting. just smile. leif doesn't even get to experience everyday squabbles with b; they are never considered a couple like babsi and roland, sebastian and magdalena, aki and tita. leif and b won't get around to savoring their difficulties. for that, they would have to come out in the open, not stay apart at all costs; they would have to feel for the other's hand not just in private, would have to be able to laugh at the stares, laugh together, kiss in the movie theater, not care, be confident, say: my boyfriend. here is where the first endurance test begins, not in the no-entry-zone of b's childhood bedroom. the fact that they can't bear each other's caresses even here shows how far the contempt of the human race extends—into people themselves. who wants to dance with me? you decide. happiness doesn't come for free, happiness still has to be fought for: we know this. sleep, sleep, dream. they are dancing. women are dancing, holding each other's hands, happily dancing in kindergarten, singing: who's afraid of the big, bad cock? nobody!! and if it creeps up on us? then we'll smash it! and the giant phallus rising above them trembles, falls, and lies smashed on the street, and b laughs; he laughs his longing, liberatingly absurd laugh: i love myself, i hate myself, i'm waking up.

half past three. lea comes home from work, wakes him, makes coffee, and they discuss chotjewitz's new book. in the neighboring village, lirus throws on a jacket, fumbles for his car keys, looks at the clock, he's going to be early, calls upstairs: see you, i'll be back at around six, i hope! and someone sticks their head briefly over the banister and says quietly, good luck and don't let them get to you. the school principal locks up his house. werner and rolf from the gay men's group sit on the train in silence. mr garrett loudly tells his wife to be quiet while he helps her into her coat: we're going to stay factual and objective, seeing as they've invited us especially! she teases a few hair-sprayed curls with the metal handle of her comb, briskly clacks into leif's room, strokes her almost eighteen-year-old son's hair with fleeting, rare tenderness, and says: isn't this the best way? you don't have to upset yourself, darling, and when we get back, this whole awful matter will be over and done with! and as if she feels compelled to find evidence of her son's innocence, her gaze wanders almost dreamily around his stylish yellow bedroom, decorated with motorbike posters. laura picks up the receiver and puts it down again without using it, then screams at her younger brother for no reason. it's now half past three, and middle-class cars almost fill the school yard, and a few teachers stand shivering next to them, and lea walks quickly through them. everyone squeezes into the teachers' lounge because it's cozier there, says the school principal, and leif doesn't feel well, says mrs garrett, and won't be in school tomorrow. outside the red-brick building, some of those who will decide b's fate smile at him as he stands with werner and rolf, and he doesn't know what they mean by it: is it solidarity expressed as tacit understanding, as it wouldn't do to show it, or pity, merely expressed by stares—or do they want to hug him? b suddenly feels irrepressibly happy, and if he doesn't stop himself, he'll burst out laughing, but he doesn't want to cry when he usually can't. this is the end of something, b knows, but what's to come is unclear, it'll just be different. at that moment, the wind blowing through the big schoolyard gets trapped in the metal trash can and whistles. those walking past the group and into the teachers' entrance feel intimidated by them. lat gets out of his car—even in the afternoon he doesn't park on the school yard, a stickler for rules—comes toward them, and doesn't manage to ignore them. lat doesn't greet or see b, only his henna-dyed pals, who are new, and his mechanical nod, directed at b, is intended for the two strangers: the one bearded, permed, and in yoga pants, the other short-haired, pointy-shoed, and decked out in fashionable beige. and unconsciously lat silently wonders: who am i dealing with here? what else should i be assessing for my pedagogical mission? even after he's walked past, his eyes are still fixed on them, until they dart back into a resting position. what do we call this? asks the biology teacher and b knows the answer: nystagmus! that's correct. sit down. nobody says anything. b watches the participants whispering as if at a funeral where people adjust their behavior to the atmosphere, so as to get it over and done with as quickly as possible. scheming erna, despite her nickname, forgets to scheme, and, in an inconspicuously conspicuous way, looks for b among the crowd of teachers on the entrance steps. one of her constant victims is lirus, a bearded man who became a teacher in the era before radicals were banned from teaching because he wants to achieve something here, and who sometimes reads marcuse in class, calling his weary introduction to economics "political economy," introducing all kinds of deviants into his courses: böll, degenhardt, krechel, mann. these teachers are the avant-garde. their liberal, hairy chests are still weak and chauvinistic, and their methods are unpopular and indiscriminate, and super democratic: you guys decide what you want to learn! they earnestly discuss reforms suggested on cdu stickers for standardized grades, are helpless and undiplomatic, call the youth of today by their first names, and are outwardly ironic and proletarian, and sofuckingleftist but: ahead of their time. are you hatching unchaste thoughts? here you go! here's a birth doula, who still uses forceps the old-fashioned way or lets the baby slide out the modern way, and wants to do the right thing. lirus will pass regulations, or enforce and represent them as head of the restructured high school of the future. he's the one who doesn't know why b's affair should be anyone's business, and shrugs and shakes his head while riding out the storm; he's the one who ended the tutors' meeting as soon as the facts were established. he has handed over the verdict to the school committee because he cannot take on this task, because he cannot do what his colleagues do, and to b, he's useless. he's useless against the garretts, their son, the infamous local newspaper, lat, and all the families. b can't pretend there's freedom where there is none. liberalism as a teaching method: sure! but: facing a machine that's crushing you, it's suicide. b shouts, i want to point the finger at these morals, at least do that while i still can. he says this sitting in lirus' living room on his large flower-patterned couch. the pair of men standing next to b will make a flyer later today, and they will hand it out in front of the school tomorrow. and even if b can't share their enthusiasm for this campaign, he loves the men's group for what it represents, which he's been lucky to learn early on: camaraderie, laid-backness, promiscuity. we're everywhere! we're the future!, b shouts on the street in front of his school, but only inwardly, keeping his face rigid as it starts to scrunch up, and then he turns away and goes inside. werner and rolf sit down on the school bench; they'll silently accompany him afterwards. b takes a seat next to lea who's already waiting for him. the teachers are gathered, still chatting, lighting cigarettes, missing their coffee which usually makes them talkative, and are even pleasant and murmuring. b knows all about these meetings because he is a student representative on the school committee and on the german faculty, and so he's seen his teachers fighting for positions—at least openly on these occasions. they correct papers on the side, or frantically keep track of their own stupidity, shouting loud "excuse mes?" across the room. and lenkel is fifteen minutes late, showing off her dress, a new one. and preuße, whom she sits next to, is hard of hearing, so she constantly has to repeat what the speaker's saying. and that's how it is today, too, amplified by confusion and murmuring, lessened perhaps by the conspicuous bloc of critical thinkers that occasionally shows up at these events, and who will be resolute today, or so b hopes. it's good that b knows all this; leif would be nervous and unable to speak and would not understand that this meeting will be absurd and sad like they always are: a gathering of relatively educated people, an elite of mini-intellectuals, b thinks disparagingly. günter schitt: the name says it all!, proud of what he's written, smiling condescendingly at obscenities. he's an artist, schitt, yesyes, didn't you know? sponsored a literary prize, didn't you hear? and even zar, the cynical historian, is tolerated by them, but then he's not in the trade union. the air outside is probably crisp and nice and cheery; in here, i'll only be able to speak while having a choking fit. the future is born into a reality in which we cannot breathe. long live self-pity! the teachers who have reason to pity themselves keep quiet because these committee meetings are not decisive. terrorization through politics, and so on, is only worthwhile when it comes to concrete issues, which are the starting point for general issues: experimental games are used to prove open-mindedness, fighting over overhead projectors kicks off a discussion on federal policy, and the middle-school syllabus is the basis for pedagogy itself. there is no requirement to learn what goes on in students' heads, so it takes them years to detangle the smallest things from their own repression: that shouting is ridiculous, for example. none of the old idealism is left. lea laughs, b asks why, she says: i just thought of my school days. everyone who has survived this stage of life leaves their negative memories behind, and repeats the same old droll stories and anecdotes when prompted: an inexhaustible treasure trove. even—or especially?—teachers have distorted views of how close everyone was, or simply their own indisputable closeness to others. b also catches himself making untenable claims about things he's too close to: e.g. the state of affairs in hospitals is clear! or: i hate my mother. soon, there'll be a musical in which everyone does an upbeat number, swaying back and forth, before they walk home: down with the education minister! solidarity for students and parents! no to the reactionary philology association! socialism for schools! b feels almost upbeat, too, now that the façade of superiority is crumbling so outrageously onto the expensive carpet, donated by the pharmacist for his son's good school-leaving grades, and mr zar the cynic grins at him, doodling stick men on his notepad as usual. what are ten years, after all, in the history of the world? and the sons are all named after some german kaiser. suddenly b's art teacher is congratulated on his baby daughter, and is given a bunch of carnations. i hate him. we've named her kathrin. now, dear colleagues, begins the principal in an awkward, quiet tone, you know the agenda for today's meeting. last reprieve, b thinks, now they're going to drag out their admin so that there is no official record of an extraordinary committee meeting: this scandal is not a scandal. after the agenda has been passed, b shuts his ears to debates about some new building in some or other school. yes, someone even dares to raise a question on this topic, and b, like everyone else, feels agitated by this tactless delay from an insensitive teacher and his observations on building plans and floor plans and notice boards and recommended usage and division heads, and—idiots, b now thinks. one huge idiot is the man sitting across from b, his biology teacher, who, right on schedule, had something to say about behavioral theory this semester. he quoted not just popular unscientific publications like *quick*, *bravo*, and *readers digest*, but also drew heavily on his own socialization, which did not contradict these in any way. desmond morris, the human zoo, quote: "like mal-imprinting, it fixes the individual onto an abnormal object, channeling sexual behavior away from the biologically normal object, namely a member of the opposite sex"! just a few hours before the school committee meeting, the biology teacher looks b in the eye and says: i believe it is important to develop an understanding of these people who just can't help the way they are; on the other hand, i can't promote it as a way of life when the interests of society take priority—the survival of the species must be upheld! this is no longer cabaret. this is dumbing-down; natural sciences reduced to the realm of anecdotes which, when lined up, result in a worldview of dull gags and exasperation. and every objection, of course, reduces your grades. in b's evaluation at the end of the semester, it says: while he added his views to the discussion, and occasionally approached the subject from a different angle, did it help the class? and the class remains silent, like it always does. this man is just a normal guy, if a little over-anxious in the way he presses his thin, greasy, wavy black hair to his semi-bald head when he gets worked up about sticklebacks; and he's a family man, of course, two kids, barely forty, and not gross or slimy or fat. wow, who'd have thought this is the way it all still functions! all this bullshit about values and norms that's constantly drummed into them like religion, this knee-jerk contempt of everything that's different. just crawl out of your urban holes, folks, and see: the asshole of the world is so close! in history class, student one is giving a talk: the nsdap was founded by a certain a dot drexler in bavaria. class: laughter. student two: what was his first name? student one: not adolf. student three: hitler, right? student four: he got married later on. student five: or strauss? student one: huh? but *his* name starts with an s? what remains of schoolday memories is a nasty aftertaste and a feeling of having wasted time. because learning happens accidentally if you don't leave behind a trail of slime from textbooks read in advance, constant homework at the ready, obedient smiles to greet teachers and notetaking. every stab at independence is suffocated by choleric teachers whose response to errors in comma rules is a partial heart attack or a drop in grades, which induces the same kind of panic as the falling dollar on the news. why is the kid next to b happy when a terrorist is shot, and why does the audience curse when stocks crash, and why is a student upset when a teacher thinks he's an idiot? all it takes is for the bighead at the front to crack his whip and shout *allez-oop!*, to click his fingers, and they all leap for grades and points through burning tires and classes, defending their choice of course at breaktime with: it makes no difference which teacher puts me down. b says farewell at this point; the principal addresses his dear fellow colleagues and it makes no difference what they decide to do. b looks at their glasses and beards and perms and fingernails and the red of their ink; he looks at these teachers, who keep on repeating cocky answers for hours, smiling, of course, and completely unmoved but deeply upset. it is disgusting how easily they can be written off in subclauses. it reveals a profession that is constantly subject to external pressure, which they pass down because they have long since internalized it. what remains? there's no solidarity: it is prevented by deep wounds on both sides. those emerging from this fight, with ringing slaps around the head and silenced, are damaged. in the same way that physical floggings produce the idiocy they claim to combat, stress and inhumanity yield work machines and self-destructive robots. they fit in. they grin at the boss's banter, only to take it out on the janitor. so, it's a fight against mockery for failure, against being written off; don't stand out, take minutes, and learn by rote. it's indoctrination through inhumanity, perfection enhanced by the experience of the rapist. on command, everyone points their right thumb down at him in the arena; b looks at the uncomprehending, dumb, possibly sad looks of the teachers. only a few are happy to be standing in the last row, not having to participate in this barbaric circus show. my dear fellow colleagues, announces the principal, we have now come to our last point on today's agenda. everyone in the room clears their throat as if a curtain is being raised. please forgive me for forgetting at the start to introduce doctor and mrs garrett, and mrs massari and her son, both of whom you probably know from sight because they are normally here as parent and student representatives. the incident, with which we are all familiar, not least of all via internal school reports, requires an objective evaluation. although we are all likely to roughly know the facts, i would ask you to keep your opinions to yourselves until the end of each presentation. i believe that nothing should stand in the way of an objective discussion. i will now give the floor to mr lirus, the tutor of the student in question and the organizer of the senior grade school trip, which is the first thing we will discuss today. as you know, both boys are students in the first semester of their senior year. mr lirus, over to you. now all eyes are on lirus and he struggles to his feet, a cliché of himself, and then clears his throat. what a shame: his average, chubby frame cannot hold itself upright, but to make up for it, he's wearing a suit, looks professional and is actually very composed. nobody knows that lirus' speech was decided in advance although there wasn't much to decide. because, of course, lirus is telling the truth, if there is one after all interpretations, jokes, defamations, and opinions have been removed. this is how i'll handle it, lirus revealed to b on his flowered couch: this incident is not an incident to speak of. what happened between you both on the trip is beyond my area of responsibility. b thinks: the only thing he's forgetting to mention is that contraception was not mandatory. lirus says: how you behaved, how the two of you behaved, is totally comprehensible. we're fortunate that comprehensible behavior is not criminal behavior in this case. now he's even making jokes. so, my report will be free of negative and! positive sentiments, which can only benefit you given how tense the situation is. the fact that you wanted these proceedings, this meeting, already proves your innocence. however, we must be under no illusions about the mood among the teaching staff. the principal will try not to lock horns with anyone and, as the idiom already suggests, especially not with the male teachers. he would sooner let scheming erna and other conservatives trample him than cross any of them. so, in front of the parents, students, and more tolerant staff members, we have to appear convincing, reflective, and calm. which we are, b adds, laughing to himself, and then says: you know what? from now on, i'm going to call you lib. why? as in gay lib. they laugh, and lirus liberalis of love bravely mans his post. in defense of the shared showers, he maintains that there was no commotion, either inwardly or outwardly. the fact that the lovers remained silent out of fear is presented as an advantage; every small act of conformity is rewarded, as is every occasion on which he holds back his outrage for the prigs just being prigs after all. lennart is giving definitions: morality is when someone fails to perceive immorality. what lirus is doing: running with the pack to run away from it— this is a pack of lies. b leans back and decides to be in favor of his tactics because sticking to his own opinion at all costs would be the feeblest compromise he could have made. lirus mentions good grades: in math, b is the worst, and in german, the top of the class, whereas with leif, it's the reverse. b goes bright purple trying to contain his hilarity: a dream couple! b can almost physically sense lirus' confidence turning into embarrassment; all eyes turn to b when he snorts. and suddenly, b feels calm. he has a realization: all of this is revolting and forced and horrifying and pointless. but lirus, they will say, tried his best and did everything within his whatchamacallit.

yet it is clear: not showing emotion is essentially taking a side. this tribunal will be a lesson—even for the slowest in the room—in how everything is biased, in how every formulation and incident involves subjectivity. how helpless are those who govern b? how absurd is this committee meeting? b learns at school: i can talk and complain and have free periods and play democracy with speakers of all classes. but b is never elected as one, although he turns up to the administrative meetings, shoots his mouth off, is always in the spotlight, acquires notoriety, is proud of his flowery trousers, his scarf, his affectations. a freak! people murmur and elect him to some position or other. the commentary lirus is now giving does not matter. the only important thing is what i now say, as it will impact everyone and shape their decision. lirus could say: we must not forget that, according to the curriculum, our teaching is supposed to be emancipatory in nature. and even if my opinion differs from some colleagues gathered here, i believe that this includes teaching our students to be open when it comes to sexual intercourse, to not feel guilty or be afraid that they will be found out, whether they are hetero- or homosexual! it's more likely that lirus will say: if we want to do justice to the phenomenon we are facing, we have to accept the specifics of the incident. in other words, we have to accept that the student leif garrett has returned to normal sexual conduct, but this does not permit us to condemn b. there is also no reason for us to intervene because the relationship is now over! or he could say nothing, or a mixture of all this, or could just drop in a few phrases about emancipation, and sit back down. heckling will not occur in any of these scenarios. the conservative bloc relies on its members to be relieved and moved, and those who agree stay just as quiet. i'm going to berlin, says b, tilting his head to one side and blinking as if he's staring at the sun. will you come with me? and ansgar smiles his lovely, silent smile and shakes his head. au revoir. let things happen for a change. take a look at the small town and say farewell. the gravel square b is walking across will soon be built over with a supermarket and an underground parking lot, and the small town will become a satellite of the big city once and for all. but for now, the small photographer's studio is still here, with his sterile color portrait of his son playing a dumb violin, and proudly retouched photos of provincial actors from the second-rate city theater. but somehow b likes it anyway. two grannies walking towards him stare openly without saying a word. idiot kids in the lower school yell at him when he leaves the school grounds at lunchtime and laugh silent insults at him when they cycle past in the afternoons. the butcher's wife is often staring out through the big shop window, and b says hello and sometimes smiles at her because she's known him since he was a boy. i'm not the only one. b's math teacher is now called upon to speak; she stands up. her teaching is fair and personal, and she leaves out all the methods that are student-unfriendly, which means her classes are packed. rather than evaluating their willingness to participate—which means punctuality and cleanliness and saying good morning—she assesses class papers and contributions to class discussions instead. instead of being evident, these things are vanishingly rare. they find expression, for instance, in her well-planned lessons, without which meaningful instruction is impossible. lirus' sloppiness is not democratic; his helpless announcements before each grading panel create sham decisions, which goes even further in its implications than the students' committee: if i want, i'll give myself high grades, if i want, i'll give great lessons, if i want, all this bullshit will be abolished, i want. let it rain good grades on me. the middle-aged math teacher now standing in front of him, whose only jewelry is a hair slide, who always wears trousers and who doesn't use "dr" in front of her name because it's not important, can also give good grades, but they are good grades of a different kind: without pressure to succeed, without grudgingly completed homework, without harassment after missed classes. she is allowed to be on the staff council because nobody else wants the position. she says: i've only known b for half a year and he's not one of my strong students, that's for sure. but still, i believe that—b looks down, hands folded over his head, and stops listening. please don't listen to her, he thinks, and: none of you deserve it. it's only worth hating people you've loved. i've never loved any of you, how could i? he laughs, looks up at the row of his german teachers, made longer by course selections and repeated tenth grades. then there are the minor subject teachers, educated to the point of stupidity, like all of them: paperbacks are going up in price, well, seven eighty won't make a difference. they consider this student a failure. zero points for the survival of the species. and when someone suspects what he's going to do, he'll do it anyway. he is calm, or only conventionally outraged, so not at all. extinct. b sits on the train to berlin, shows his passport and a tired face. staying in the small town with mommy dear? that's not the solution. yes, you all embraced me. but you also got me to cross my arms. you brought me up, dear people. and i need you after all. you are very close to me now because i have nothing left to lose. in an unspectacular scene, leif's father offloads his moral judgement painlessly and bluntly, demanding b's expulsion from the school. b knows that lenkel voted against this motion even though he does not witness it. when she calls him back afterwards, he can tell from the way she looks at him. neither of them cry, and yet they do. and i still need you. you guys, I was kicked out! i could cry because i am free. free for the taking, on the free market. for sale: gay high-school student without money for boarding school looking for meaningful work. yes, nurse adelgard, becoming a nurse is the most direct way to help people. besides: who else will take me? besides: gays become window dressers, booksellers, or nurses because those are the most humane jobs. besides: b's experience of free choice is the opposite. it is absurd to retreat into a private life that's only allowed to exist because it contributes to public life. the decision for or against leif is no decision, just as being for or against the world is not one either. my experiences and my people exist, advertising and schools exist, therefore i exist: socialization. and therefore, leif exists. who was a man, above all else. fallen in the daily battle. in the future, losses on both sides are expected. war, farewell. in the restaurant car of the train sits a man, around forty, with his mother. they are eating schnitzel with salad, and clearly know each other very well, familiar beyond recognition. every scrap of a sentence produces habitual reactions, marked by the habitual tone of their voices, gestures, and looks. they live together, b thinks, or see each other very often. and: they have no choice either. a mute show of give and take, of casseroles and compliments, of annoyances and apple strudel. i don't want to become like that, b thinks, and makes an effort to seem as disinterested as possible. at least there's choice in running away, in making a decision: stay or make a brave new start. those who don't realize before it's too late that remaining at home with mother does not lead to happiness end up like this pair: getting up, making coffee, looking in the mirror a whole life long, orders, warnings, instructions, all sickeningly important. the paradox of staying together and going crazy cannot be resolved. border number two: mother. i am happy i have you, lea. but still: farewell. for i will still be your son when i am forty. i am b, not just your son. i will learn to cut the nails of my right hand on my own. i will be b without you. i will learn to talk to you after the cinema about the movie. now it's b's turn, because lea wants to stay silent. new roles, new town. farewell. being able to say yes to oneself and one's past. being able to say no to those who were brought up differently. tolerance? but self-confidence. it is enough to make your own way without needing everyone's approval. and without illusions: no life is enough to change circumstances all by yourself. being able to learn. with others and for them. no longer afraid of groups, no longer afraid: a dream, but true. melancholy is more righteous than anger. b feels on edge, and so smiles confidently. stands up. i am getting closer to the future. bahnhof zoo, the end of the line. nice beginning, in a heap of dirt. the ability to search. the desire for subculture? that too, and the realization: that there is no happiness here and now. whoever knows this lets contradictions stand and concentrates on what's feasible, has a future. the contradiction of leif and b, the contradiction of lea and b, the contradiction of the world and happiness. what's possible: to never give up striving for happiness, an idea of love even now in this stone age. for as long as people's relationship to their work, neighbors, and themselves is self-destructive, the queers won't be an exception either. i embraced leif, that's all. i won't hold off from embracing the world. i will no longer be knocked down by people who have stories, like i have mine. i will always keep trying to love. i will no longer try to run away from embraces. i will live in embraces, that's what i want. i will only be able to live and work if i don't try to avoid embraces and if i try to change the world. b dances tonight like it's a vacation, not a solution, and the doors to a thousand underworlds open for him: from the youth club to the punk bakery hangout, from a squat to the countryside, from the small town to berlin. and now, under the station clock, all his lovers, and everyone he will love in the future are gathered: the drag queen from tv, from aznavour's chanson, from exotic parts of berlin, they all embrace him, from near and far, and smiling in the background, there's his english teacher and leif. lenkel smooths her checked dress. lirus chews the little strip between his upper lip and beard, lost in thought. the principal rifles through his papers without looking at him. someone whispering in his neighbor's ear a moment earlier hushes. the geography teacher stops drawing. b runs his fingers through his hair. lea stares at her fingernails, her hands on her knees. zar's earnestness now gives b courage. dear fellow students. eckart and liane look at him. he can cry in laura's arms, just think of her and doing that. what if laura had not kept quiet? if you love me, it's all or nothing. the sound keeps cutting out and people keep lowering their eyes. groups give brave looks, individuals turn away. footsteps. parents' representatives. garrett stifles the need to clear his throat and corrects the knot of his tie below his red face. walking in berlin, going forwards. here the group stood, laughing. small suitcase now, subway, the address of a gay men's group. berlin versions of werner and rolf. underworlds and dancing. teachers. i embrace you.

Afterword
by Ben Miller

The longest work of gay literature—*In Search of Lost Time*, by Marcel Proust—begins with an adolescent falling asleep. He tosses and turns, reflecting on the day past. "A sleeping man," he writes, "holds in a circle around him… the order of the years and worlds. He consults them instinctively as he wakes and reads in a second the point on the earth he occupies, the time that has elapsed before his waking; but their ranks can be mixed up, broken." Sixty-six years later, to open one of the shortest book-length works of gay literature—the newly translated *SMALLTOWNNOVELLA*, by Ronald M. Schernikau—an adolescent wakes up, broken. Much has elapsed before his waking. He embraces himself, comes to in bed before a day of school he's dreading.

Andrew Holleran once described male homosexuality as "a boarding school at which there are no vacations." The alternatingly brutal and tender entanglements of privileged schoolboys, and the men they eventually become, fill the pages of gay literature. Most faggots are working class, yet gay literature has been mainly interested in boarding schools, and the penthouses, and discos which the boarding school faggots fill after graduation. Alternately, these novels track the self-exile of the gay bourgeoisie into chic lofts, where they await the civil rights that make those lofts more valuable speculative assets than their parents' Dutch Colonials ever were. (Many of these novels, it must be said, are among my favorite works of literature. The bourgeoisie, to which I belong, has its discreet charms.)

From the beginning, a counter-literature including writers as different as Leslie Feinberg and James Baldwin has explored queer lives as they are actually lived by most people, which is to say without enough money and in cramped apartments. This work understands homo- and transsexuality as the question of what people made strange by systems of sex and gender can teach us about how those systems create everyone, and how sex-gender systems are themselves co-constituted with systems of production, exchange, and racialization. Now, thanks to the work of Lucy Jones, Ronald

M. Schernikau takes his place in an Anglophone understanding of that counter-literature.

Schernikau was born in 1960 in Magdeburg, in East Germany. When he was six, his mother Ellen smuggled him across the border into the West. They were planning on joining his father, who had fled to the neighboring West German province of Lower Saxony. Upon arrival, Ellen discovered that Ronald's father was married and had become a neo-Nazi. She raised Ronald as a single mother in a Lower Saxon town called Lehrte. West Germany in the mid-1960s had not yet built its social welfare state. The twenty years after the war had seen Germany ruled by the grim-faced Konrad Adenauer and his cabinets full of ex-Nazis. Adenauer's motto was "*No experiments.*" His preferred solution to male homosexuality was imprisonment: he sent more gay men to prison for sodomy than the Nazis had, with some even sent back to jail directly from concentration camps. His preferred response to the Holocaust was silence. His preferred explanation for how the Nazis had come to power was public immorality and excessive indebtedness. The country he built in his image was provincial and reactionary, especially in matters of sex and gender. East German women, even in the context of Stalinist dictatorship, had significantly more freedom to work, to abort, and to live self-determined lives than West German women, who were expected to be dutiful housewives.

A poor single mother in West Germany and her effeminate son were therefore the objects of pity, derision, and aggression, especially when the young Ronald defied his class position by winning admission to a German "gymnasium," or grammar school. The German educational system remains tuition-free through the post-graduate level. Nevertheless, complex mechanisms of social control ensure that the country has less social mobility than places where education costs money. While still in primary school, students are split into different educational tracks. Only those selected for "gymnasium" are eligible to study at university. Everyone else is sent into the trades. This system neatly reproduces existing social hierarchies while allowing Germans to conceive of their society as meritocratic.

Another gymnasium student in Lehrte at the time was a young woman named Ursula Albrecht. An heiress, the great-granddaughter of South Carolina slavers and Hanseatic cotton merchants, she was also, by the time the two were finishing school, the daughter of the governor of Lower Saxony. She entered politics, became a confidante of Angela Merkel, and served in her cabinets. In 2019, she was appointed to the Presidency of the European Commission. This was the type of student the Lehrte Gymnasium was intended to educate. When Schernikau writes of CDU keychains on low-slung jeans, he may well be describing a teenaged Ursula von der Leyen.

Gymnasiums are, in theory, intended to impart a comprehensive humanistic education, what Germans call *Bildung*. Alexander von Humboldt described *Bildung* as "the linking of the self to the world." *Bildung* could also be a noun describing the massacre of the spirit necessary to transform a human child into a German adult. *Bildung*, in midcentury West Germany, was intended to create a type of man (some, like the young Ursula, took advantage of social transformations their class bitterly opposed in order to become this type of woman) who would wield power and influence in the new transatlanticist capitalist order. The term *Bildungsroman*, a German word for novels of education and development—tales of children becoming adults—survives untranslated in English. *SMALLTOWNNOVELLA* is a novella of both kinds of *Bildung*: both the linking of the self to the world and the institutional destruction of feeling necessary to produce subjects who will manage and govern.

"i wrap my arms around myself," says the narrator, b, a student; the final sentence reads, "i embrace you." The fractured self is made whole; through an education, the self is linked to the world. This education, though, has little to do with the dull school lessons. No saintly, handsome literature teacher inspires this schoolboy to greatness in a mahogany-paneled library pregnant with confused desire and significant glances. Instead, the narrator receives an education in how the world actually works—in who it is designed to protect, in how class is reproduced, in how boys become men, and in how to use the system to try to seed its destruction. The crucial stylistic decision to write in all lowercase lends the English-language text an air of 1970s informality but in German does something even more radical. German nouns are all capitalized: objects cruise through a sea of description and action like Prussian battleships in the Baltic Sea. Forcing everything into lowercase has the effect of confusing objects and actions. It emphasizes process; it radically destabilizes.

Lowercase prose is only one of the stylistic choices and structural considerations that make *SMALLTOWNNOVELLA* both formally rigorous and satisfying. Hopefully, paired with Schernikau's undeniable political commitments, this experimental yet rigorous engagement with craft can help put to bed the twinned vapid arguments that, on the one hand, 'craft' is complicit with the systems of violence and destruction that govern our world, and, on the other, that there is currently 'too much politics' in literature and art. Craft is an ethically neutral tool. Killing people, taking their land, and building a house on it is a crime. The craft of house-building, however, is not complicit in that crime. Why should we assume there is something radical about doing things badly, or that there is something politically suspect about the architectural precision of a well-executed sentence or a poem? It is because we can describe that we should endeavor to describe well—and this includes a consideration of the ideologies of form, and the awareness that the writer cannot simply free themself from their context. Equally reactionary is the discourse about overly political art and literature, the privileging of apolitical literatures as more complex or worthy of praise—that whole sloppy midbrow critical apparatus that Tobi Haslett has diagnosed with "a McCarthyist... boredom with social critique."

Both of these positions posit a supposed opposition between political commitment and aesthetic values. They depend on parched concepts of both politics and aesthetics and, in confusing the two for one another, prevent us from understanding either. People love mentioning Kurt Weill's aside to Berthold Brecht that he "[could] not set the Communist Manifesto to music," but neglect to mention that Erwin Schulhoff did so in 1932, and rather well. If politics are aesthetics—if we confuse the look and feel of resistance with the actual labor of organizing, which has a lot to do with craft, in its own way—then nothing is politics, and nothing is aesthetics either. We rob ourselves both of our ability to act and to create, of our ability to organize and to describe.

Schernikau knew that literary creation and political engagement are intimately related in unpredictable ways. He knew this despite being taught that "all the political writers were awful, with no exceptions." Part of *Bildung* as conceived of by a school designed to produce Ursula von der Leyen is the division of art from politics, the enshrinement of artistic production in a separate sphere from the material. Part of *Bildung* as Schernikau's narrator conceives of it is learning that this view of literature is impoverished, insufficient, and fundamentally useless.

No, this narrator's *Bildung* doesn't come from the school's lessons. Even the progressive teachers at the half-reformed school come in for a mix of pity and scorn; lirus, a "beardy-weirdy who... sometimes reads marcuse in class" stands in for a weak, fundamentally liberal avant-garde; "liberalism as a teaching method: sure! but: facing a machine that's crushing you, it's suicide." Teachers at the Lehrte Gymnasium convey disembodied facts. "if people never learn about contexts," b asks, "how can they assume there were any?"

Formal education is part of the machine; rather than connecting the self to the world, b perceives it distancing, separating, removing:

> what remains? there's no solidarity: it is prevented by deep wounds on both sides. those emerging from this fight, with ringing slaps around the head and silenced, are damaged. in the same way that physical floggings produce the idiocy they claim to combat, stress and inhumanity yield work machines and self-destructive robots. they fit in.

With chilling concision, Schernikau describes the function of locker-room banter: "this is where men are trained to beat up faggots and rape women. this is where the systematic destruction of happiness takes place." The narrator perceives both the violence that this form of masculinity, part of official West German *Bildung*, will do to the world it will govern, as well as the violence it does to its perpetrators. The narrator separates himself from these men, desires these men, refuses their fate. The boy he briefly loves refuses his embrace, refuses his invitation to a different life, returns to his fate: "what leif can expect from life is blissful normality, achieved by doing nothing, no matter what."

In 1992, Monique Wittig wrote that "lesbians are not women"; in 2024, Kay Gabriel wrote that "faggots are women." Schernikau also perceives this:

> b is feeling under pressure and when a nurse from the hospital boasts of her new hairdo: the competition never sleeps, b laughs, unnaturally loudly, realizing: that's me, forced to play along, i'll never get anything in life for free. [...] don't accuse gays of acting unreasonably in an unreasonable world! what's the difference between a thirty-six-year-old gay man and an eighteen-year-old girl? when it comes to innocence and its opposite? what b sees in the discos of both scenes is shockingly similar.

Patriarchy must be engaged with rather than simply refused: being gay won't exempt b from men's violence, or from their desire, or from his desire for them.

The friend with whom b falls in love is named leif garrett. Leaving aside the compact poesis of this name choice—one can't read that name without thinking of the angel-faced, blond-locked teen idol, and his embodiment of the long-haired, pouty masculinity of the late 1970s and early 1980s—the boy is presented as an unremarkable product of the class and sex-gender systems of the time. Their dalliance is understood by everyone involved—from b, to leif's shocked parents, to the school authorities whose intervention is framed entirely around the idea that b bears the responsibility for what occurred, that he corrupted leif's morals—as a temporary interruption of leif's journey to the kind of manhood that Lehrte's *Bildung* aims to construct and that Schernikau, and his narrator, see as a fate worse than death. For b, it is precisely leif's proximity to class-gender reproduction that makes him attractive: "who is leif? a member of the group, the joiner in persona, the longed-for happiness." When the narrative voice briefly enters leif's head, what it narrates is the automatism of becoming-man, and the threat that dalliance with b poses to that becoming:

> somewhere in leif's mind, this experience exists too, he knows it from his own reactions, from school, from his parents, drill is everything, everything is drill, it goes right through me. i'm seventeen and a man, and there's no need to crack the whip to teach me...what leif can expect from life is blissful normality, achieved by doing nothing, no matter what.

It is not a coincidence that leif envisions this becoming-man, this *Bildung*, in terms—"drill is everything, every thing is drill"—borrowed from Goethe's *Faust*, one of majoritarian German *Bildung*'s most revered literary texts. It is literally on these terms that leif becomes the kind of man who, dead-eyed and plundering, rules the world.

These systems and structures govern even the private lives of students. The tribunal to which b is subjected "will be a lesson—even for the slowest in the room—in how everything is biased, in how every formulation and incident involves subjectivity." There are no easy answers here. Engagement with the world on its terms doesn't precisely work: b runs for class offices and makes himself known in student politics, but never earns the respect automatically granted to a boy like leif who comes from the right kind of family and whose youthful rebellions don't threaten his *Bildung*.

Youthful rebellions are part of a subcultural '68er politics towards which the novella is in general tremendously unfriendly. Describing a classmate on his way to joining what would become the German Green Party, Schernikau writes that he is

> a progressive student who belongs to an equally progressive clique. the guy smokes dope, dyes his hair, has nothing against his neighbor's homosexuality, nothing against leftists, nothing against being sensitive or feminism... at some point, he'll have his hair cut short like all the others... if you're not a communist by seventeen, you have no heart, but if you're still one when you're thirty, you have no brains.

This precise path, from small-town autonomist youth to urban liberal, is one of the most well-trodden in German politics. As Nicolas Becker once said of the Greens, they are "opportunistic, vegetarian,

Protestant." Schernikau's narrator wears a keffiyeh in the novel; he would presumably have been disgusted by these opportunists' recent turn towards a muscularly nationalist xenophobia blaming Muslim immigrants for the Jewish blood staining Germany's hands.

And yet the novella ends in thrall to the specific subculture of gay Berlin: that's where the narrator escapes, despite knowing the escape will be incomplete. It is no use to pretend that there is anything other than the world, rather the task is to link the self to it: "it is absurd to retreat into a private life that is only allowed to exist because it contributes to public life... my experiences and my people exist, advertising and school exist, and therefore i exist: socialization." The exhilarating rush of realizations with which the novella ends, its evocation of a new life, is framed by a vision of the old life, populated by apparitions of everyone the narrator has ever loved, including leif. Even the hapless teachers from the Lehrte Gymnasium are extended this benevolent embrace.

When *SMALLTOWNNOVELLA* was published, it sold well and made Schernikau a regular TV talk show guest. He moved to West Berlin, studied German and philosophy at the Freie Universität, and joined the Sozialistische Einheitspartei Westberlins, an East German-funded and supported Communist Party. Disillusioned once again by the subcultures into which he'd fled (his later book *so schön* describes life in West Berlin's 1980s gay scene) he began writing more political journalism. The naivité of his style only intensified, as did his insistence on taking things seriously, on noticing details, even or especially when reporting on parts of the East German system that seemed the most ridiculous. In 1986, Schernikau began a two-year program of study at the East German state writers' academy in Leipzig, one of the few Westerners who would ever study there. While there, he wrote *The Days in L.: On the Fact That East Germany and West Germany Will Never Understand Each Other, Least of All Through Their Literature.* Published in West Germany by konkret, the book was too critical of the East German state to be released on the other side of the wall.

Nevertheless, in 1989, Schernikau decided to emigrate to East Germany. His citizenship was approved in September of that year. Two months later, the Wall fell. Schernikau became the last Westerner to defect. At the final conference of the East German national writers' association, Schernikau berated East German intellectuals for having accepted a Western counterrevolution as 'freedom.' He warned that the capitalist system, free from competition or threat, would demand "subjugation...from every single one of its inhabitants" that even subjects of dictatorship could not comprehend. Then, he died.

He died, in October 1991, of AIDS-related illness. The diagnosis came only after his emigration to the East. As a politically-engaged gay writer, Schernikau had tangled with the crisis: his two most famous essays about it are entitled "fickt weiter" ("keep fucking"), a 1984 polemic urging gays to not allow the crisis to separate them from their sexual liberation, and the more sombre essay "das personal" ("the staff"), a touching exploration of the lifeworlds of the doctors, nurses, and patients at an AIDS ward in a Munich hospital. When he died, he left behind *legende* (*legend*), a ten-part, thousand-plus page magnum opus.

Five of the book's ten parts, *legende* proper, focus on the inhabitants of "The Island," a fictionalized West Berlin which, like the real city, sat "like an egg yolk" in the middle of a foreign country. This Island is ruled over by gods (Klaus Mann, Ulrike Meinhof, Therese Giehse, and Max Riemann), and the text is written in biblical form, in books, chapters, and verses. The other five chapters, presented as 'inserts' into the main text, are various unrelated texts Schernikau was unable to publish in his lifetime, including *Irene Binz*, a consideration of his mother Ellen. The epigraph to *legende* reads:

> You must remind yourself with every self-indulgence that you find here that I was almost entirely unsuccessful for ten years when I wrote this. You must consider that I was forced to deliver my late work in my thirties. If you are reading this book, then I am famous, a stroke of art, but now! If you are reading this book, then I am already long dead. Hopefully! The times past! The joyful farewell! How funny and odd are those things which lift us above our toil.

Then, he died.

Before he died, he wrote: "the only thing that interests me is to be able to praise something. I hate negation." We may live in dark times, we may see world-historical defeats on the horizon, but we should keep living, keep fucking, keep refusing to let the light go out. Writing and thinking well are not acts of resistance any more than subculture is automatically resistant. They are not sufficient—but they are certainly necessary. I embrace you.

Ronald M. Schernikau was born in 1960 in Magdeburg, East Germany and grew up in Lehrte, a small town near Hanover, West Germany. After completing his Abitur in 1980, he moved to West Berlin and studied German literature, philosophy, and psychology. In 1986, he started studying at the Institut für Literatur Johannes R. Becher (German Institute for Literature) in Leipzig, GDR. In 1989 he obtained GDR citizenship and relocated to East Berlin. He worked as a dramaturge and in radio and TV until his death of AIDS-related illness in 1991. His publications include *Kleinstadtnovelle* (*SMALL-TOWNNOVELLA*, 1980); *Die Tage in L.* (*The Days in L.*, 1989); *legende* (*legend*, 1999); *Königin im Dreck* (*Queen in the Dirt*, 2009); and *Irene Binz: Die Befragung* (*Irene Binz: The Interview*, 2010).

Lucy Jones is a British translator and writer based in Berlin. She is the translator of Brigitte Reimann's *Siblings* (Penguin Modern Classics, 2023), Anke Stelling's *Higher Ground* (Scribe, 2021) and Annemarie Schwarzenbach's *Lyric Novella* (Seagull Books, 2022), among others. Her translations and book reviews have appeared in *Asymptote*, *Words Without Borders*, and *CulturMag*. She was the runner-up for the Society of Author's Schlegel-Tieck Prize in 2023. Her own writing has been published in *SAND Journal*, *3:AM Magazine*, *Pigeon Papers NYC*, and *LitroMag*.

Ben Miller is a writer and historian living in Berlin. He is the author of *Bad Gays: A Homosexual History* (Verso, 2022) and currently at work on a biography of the fashion designer and counterculture activist Rudi Gernreich (Norton, forthcoming), as well an academic monograph about primitivism and the self-invention of the white gay man. His criticism, journalism, and fiction have appeared in, among other places, *The London Review of Books*, *The New York Times*, *The Baffler*, *The Los Angeles Review of Books*, and *Tin House.* He holds a PhD from the Graduate School of Global Intellectual History at the Freie Universität Berlin.

Ugly Duckling Presse's LOST LITERATURE Series publishes neglected, never-before-translated, or scarcely available works of poetry and prose, and resonant historical works that fall outside these confines.

1. Gabriel Pomerand, *Saint Ghetto of the Loans*
2. Vito Acconci, Bernadette Mayer, *0 to 9: The Complete Magazine*
3. Aram Saroyan, *Complete Minimal Poems*
4. Paul Scheerbart, *The Development of Aerial Militarism*
5. Su Shi, *East Slope*
6. Jack Micheline, *One of a Kind*
7. Carlos Oquendo de Amat, *5 Meters of Poems*
8. Manuel Maples Arce, *City: Bolshevik Super-Poem in 5 Cantos*
9. Guillevic, *Geometries*
10. Ernst Herbeck, *Everyone Has a Mouth*
11. Heimrad Bäcker, *Seascape*
12. Alejandra Pizarnik, *Diana's Tree*
13. César Vallejo & César González-Ruano, *Vallejo: Heraldo de Madrid*
14. Alejandra Pizarnik, *The Most Foreign Country*
15. Hirato Renkichi, *Spiral Staircase: Collected Poems*
16. Marosa di Giorgio, *I Remember Nightfall*
17. Constance DeJong, *Modern Love*
18. Eleni Vakalo, *Before Lyricism*
19. Laura Riding, *Experts are Puzzled*
20. Laura Riding, *Convalescent Conversations*
21. Marcel Duchamp, Henri-Pierre Roche, Beatrice Wood, *The Blind Man*
22. Arnaldo Calveyra, *Letters So That Happiness*

23. Omar Cáceres, *Defense of the Idol*
24. Amanda Berenguer, *Materia Prima*
25. Paul Nougé, Paul Colinet, Louis Scutenaire, *Ideas Have No Smell: Three Belgian Surrealist Booklets*
26. Alejandra Pizarnik, *A Tradition of Rupture*
27. Alejandra Pizarnik, *The Last Innocence / The Lost Adventure*
28. Laura Riding, *The Close Chaplet*
29. Bobbie Louise Hawkins, *One Small Saga*
30. Åke Hodell, *The Marathon Poet*
31. Ulises Carrión, *Sonnet(s)*
32. Susana Thénon, *Ova Completa*
33. Salette Tavares, *Lex Icon*
34. Haroldo de Campos, *galáxias*
35. N. H. Pritchard, *The Matrix*
36. Ronald M. Schernikau, *SMALLTOWNNOVELLA*

The translator's work on this text was supported by the German Translators' Fund.

Ugly Duckling Presse thanks the following sponsors for their generous support of this project: Andrew E. McDonald, Paulo Gonzalez, Rainer Diana Hamilton, and Patrick Greaney.

Book design by IngeInge and Kireji.

Cover design by Jimmy Pizza.

The type is Graveur with titles in Hardwood.

Printed & bound at Bookmobile (Minneapolis, MN)